BOOP!

Dear Booper,

All the dogs in this book want you to boop their snoots! Before you touch a <u>real</u> dog, always ask your big people and the dog's big people if it is okay.

—B.B.

BOOP!

Words by
Bea Birdsong

Pictures by
Linzie Hunter

HARPER
An Imprint of HarperCollins Publishers

This is a **snoot.**

Snoots <u>need</u> BOOPS.

Can you help boop this snoot?

A boop is a pat.
A **gentle** tap.

Get your **finger** ready and...

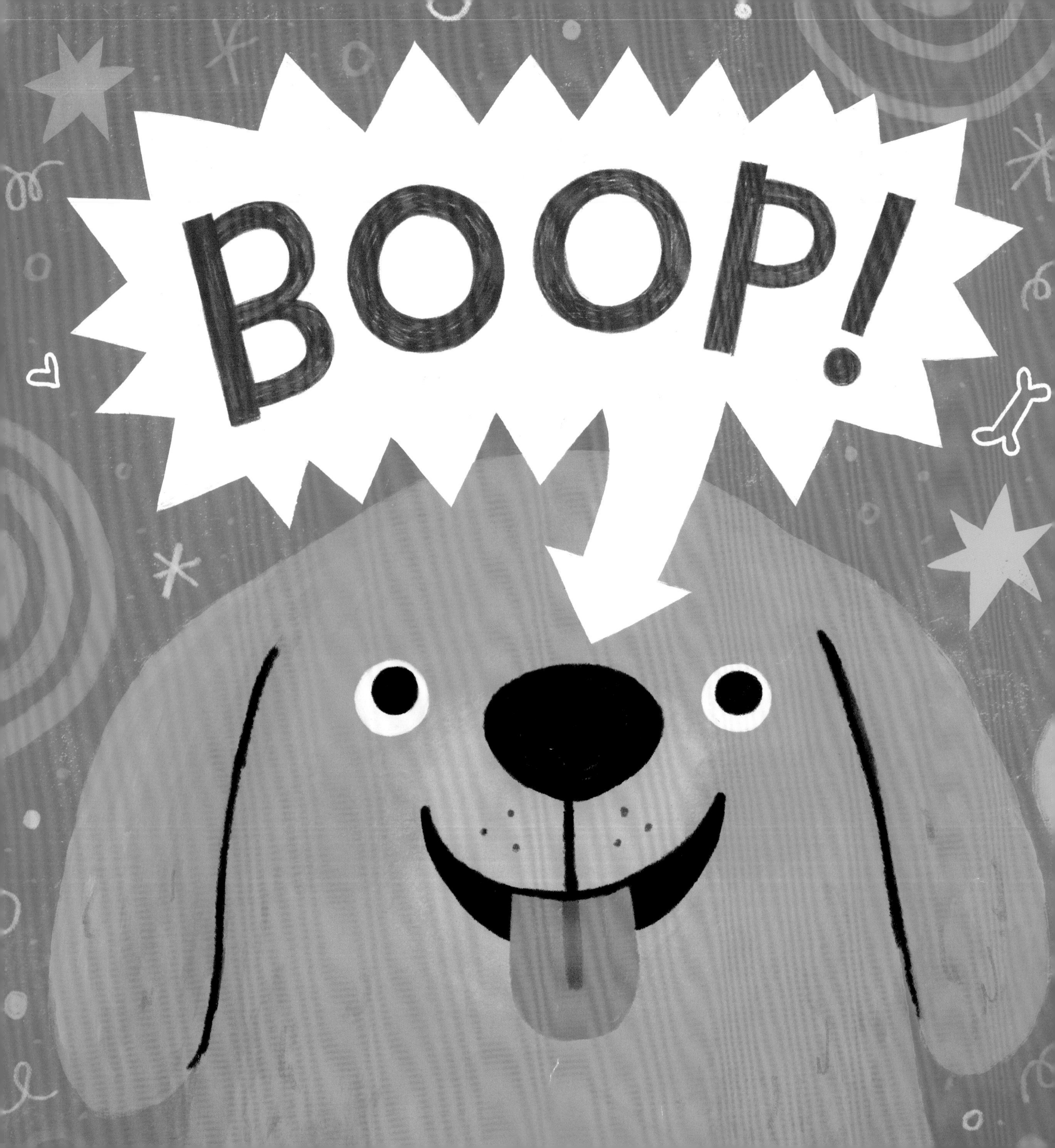
BOOP!

You booped the snoot!

Clap hands! Hooray!

And now
the <u>tail</u> will
Swish and **sway!**

Oh, look! More snoots!

One snoot.

Two snoots.

Three snoots.

Four.

A gentle tap.
A friendly pat.

Some snoots
are **big.**

Some
snoots
are small.

Some snoots have **beards**...

Let's boop them all!

Can you boop the floofiest snoot?

Can you boop the smooshiest snoot?

You are a BOOper Extraordinaire!

The boopiest booper

Biscuits

with **Booping**

FLAIR!

Uh-oh!
What's
this? →

More snoots need boops!

Sitting boop.

Standing boop.

Upside-down boop.

Around-and-around boop.

You booped **EVERY** snoot!

Clap hands! Hooray!

And now the tails will—

Wait!

STOP the BOOK!

There's **one** more snoot that needs a **boop!**

Get your finger ready

and...

Boop *

your

Snoot!

For all the dogs and the people who love them. —B.B.

For John G., an extraordinary booper, and for Connie, an excellent boopee. —L.H.

For information address HarperCollins Children's Books, a division of HarperCollins Publishers, 195 Broadway, New York, NY 10007 • www.harpercollinschildrens.com • Library of Congress Control Number: 2022935784 • ISBN 978-0-06-321480-4 • The artist used Procreate and Photoshop to create the digital illustrations for this book • 23 24 25 26 27 RTLO 10 9 8 7 6 5 4 3 2 1 • First Edition